MERCER MAYER'S
LC + THE CRITTER KIDS®

TH
HAUNTED HOUSE

A Golden Book • New York

Western Publishing Company, Inc., Racine, Wisconsin 53404

A Mercer Mayer Ltd./J. R. Sansevere Book

Copyright © 1995 Mercer Mayer Ltd. All rights reserved.
Printed in the U.S.A. No part of this book may be reproduced or
copied in any form without written permission from the publisher.
Critter Kids® is a Registered Trademark of Mercer Mayer. All other
trademarks are the property of Western Publishing Company, Inc.
Library of Congress Catalog Card Number: 94-73092
ISBN: 0-307-16180-3/ISBN: 0-307-66180-6 (lib. bdg.)   A MCMXCV

Written by Erica Farber/J. R. Sansevere

LC

VELVET

LITTLE SISTE

TIGER

KOOL BEAR

SLICK RICK

SU SU   GABBY   TIMOTHY

GATOR   FLEX   HENRIETTA

CHAPTER 1

THAT'S THE WAY THE MUFFIN CRUMBLES

LC bent down and took a deep breath. "One, two, three," he said. Then he picked up the huge stack of books piled on the floor of the Critters' den.

"Can you put the book you're reading on top?" LC asked Little Sister.

"No way," said Little Sister. "I'm reading."

Little Sister loved looking through the encyclopedia. She

planned to read every single volume, starting with the last one first.

"I need that book," said LC. "You can read it tomorrow."

"You have all those other books," said Little Sister, holding on tightly to the book. "Why do you need this one?"

"I need all of them for my research," said LC. "My report's due tomorrow."

"So why don't you just write it?" asked Little Sister.

"I will," said LC. "But I need to finish my research first. A good report is all about research."

"All right," said Little Sister. "I guess I read enough for today." She put the "XYZ" volume on top of the big stack of books LC was holding.

LC started walking slowly up the stairs.

"I feel sorry for you," said Little Sister, following him. "You've been working on your report all week and you're not done yet. You're running out of time."

LC didn't say anything. He just walked into his room and kicked the door shut.

"I bet you never finish that report!" yelled Little Sister.

LC sighed. He knew Little Sister was right. He was running out of time. His history report was due tomorrow. He hadn't even decided which famous critter to write about. And he would be in big trouble if he didn't hand it in on time.

LC dropped the books on his desk. He sat down and opened the drawer to find a pencil. He pulled out half a pack of Bananarama gum, one cracked purple marble, a ticket stub from a Critter Cubs game, some old *X-Critter* comics, and three baseball cards. There had to be a pencil somewhere. Maybe he had one in his knapsack.

LC opened his knapsack and reached inside. He found a pencil stub just big enough to use. Then he pulled out a piece of paper. It was a little wrinkled. He smoothed it out and put it on his desk.

LC chewed on the end of his eraser. Boy, he sure was thirsty. He needed a glass of

orange juice. It always helped him concentrate. Once he had a glass of orange juice, he was sure he could start his report.

LC slid down the banister. He ran into the kitchen. His mother was making dinner. Little Sister was drinking a glass of orange juice.

"How's your report going?" asked Mrs. Critter, wiping her hands on her apron.

"Excellent," said LC. "Hey, where's the orange juice?"

"We just ran out," said Mrs. Critter. "Little Sister had the last glass."

"Yep," said Little Sister, making a loud slurping sound.

"Oh, no!" said LC. "I need orange juice, or I'll never be able to finish my report."

"Why don't you get some at the market,"

said Mrs. Critter. "You can pick up a couple of tomatoes for me while you're there."

"Okay," LC said.

Mrs. Critter handed LC some money. He hopped on his bike and rode to Muncher's Market.

Su Su and Gabby, two girls in LC's class, were sitting on the steps. Gabby and LC had been friends ever since they were babies. She lived next door to him.

"Hey, LC," said Gabby. "Did you finish your report?"

"I'm working on it," said LC.

"I finished mine yesterday," said Su Su. "And my father's secretary typed it."

"Give me a break," said Gabby.

Just then a big white car pulled up in front of the market. A large lady wearing a flowered dress and a big straw hat got out.

"Hello, Miss Van der Critter," said Su Su. Then she turned to LC and Gabby. "She has the biggest house in Critterville," whispered Su Su. "And tons of antiques and jewelry worth millions and millions of dollars."

"Hello, dear," said Miss Van der Critter, smiling at Su Su. She walked slowly up the steps, leaning on her white cane. "Tell your mother I hope to see her at the charity tea at the country club this weekend."

"I'm sure she'll be there," said Su Su.

"She wouldn't miss it for anything."

"Splendid," said Miss Van der Critter, walking slowly into the store.

"Well, I better go in, too," said LC to Gabby and Su Su. "See ya later."

LC walked into the market. He went down one aisle and picked up a container of orange juice. Now, where are the tomatoes, he wondered. LC walked toward

the front of the store. He spotted them below the window. He picked out two red tomatoes that were soft but not too soft, just the way his mom liked them. He brought everything to the counter.

"Hi, LC," said Rocky, who was working at the cash register.

LC and Rocky high-fived each other. LC liked Rocky a lot. He was a senior at Critterville High and he worked at the market to earn money for college.

Right next to Rocky on the counter was something that made LC's mouth water: one huge chocolate chip muffin. LC just had to have that muffin.

MMM GOOD!

"Is that everything?" asked Rocky.

"Uh-huh," said LC. "Oh, and I'll take that chocolate chip muffin."

"Okay," said Rocky, ringing everything up.

LC picked up the muffin. He was about to take a bite when somebody tapped the counter right next to him with a long white cane. "Not so fast," said a grouchy voice. "That's *my* muffin!"

LC dropped the muffin and turned around. The voice belonged to none other than Miss Van der Critter.

"What about a cupcake instead, Miss Van der Critter?" suggested Rocky.

"How dare you?" yelled Miss Van der Critter, waving her cane in Rocky's face. "I always reserve one chocolate chip muffin every day. If you weren't so stupid, you would know that."

"B-b-but LC ju-ju-just p-paid . . ." Rocky stammered.

"Do you know who I am?" thundered Miss Van der Critter, moving her mouth up and down so fiercely that all of her chins wiggled. "My great-grandfather Cornelius Van der Critter founded this town!" she yelled. "If it wasn't for him there would be no Critterville today!"

LC's eyes lit up as he stared at Miss Van der Critter. What a great idea, he thought. He could do his report about Cornelius Van der Critter!

Just then Mr. Muncher, the owner of the market, rushed up to the counter. "Is something the matter, Miss Van der Critter?" he asked.

"Why, yes, there is!" she shouted. "This boy forgot to reserve my muffin again. I want him fired!"

LC looked from Miss Van der Critter to Rocky in surprise. Rocky couldn't get fired. He needed this job, or he'd never make enough money to go to college.

"Here's your muffin," said LC, quickly picking it up and handing it to Miss Van der Critter.

"I *don't* want it. You *touched* it!" said Miss Van der Critter. "I want this boy fired. Or I'm never setting foot in this store again."

"Miss Van der Critter . . ." began Mr. Muncher, "perhaps I could interest you in our delicious homemade brownies . . ."

"Fiddlesticks!" yelled Miss Van der Critter. "Fire this boy now—or else!"

Miss Van der Critter stamped her foot and stormed out of the store.

"I'm sorry, Rocky," said Mr. Muncher. "But Miss Van der Critter is one of our best customers and I can't afford to lose her business."

"I know," said Rocky. "It's okay."

Rocky took off his apron and walked out of the market. Poor Rocky, thought LC. Miss Van der Critter was so mean. LC wondered if Cornelius Van der Critter was as mean as his great-granddaughter. He couldn't wait to get home and start his research.

CHAPTER 2

THE GHOST OF SHADOW CLOSE

The next morning LC put his report carefully in his knapsack. He had stayed up past twelve o'clock the night before, working on it. LC picked up his knapsack and whistled as he walked downstairs and into the kitchen.

"Did you finish your history report?" asked Mrs. Critter.

"Yep," said LC. "And I think it's the best thing I ever wrote. Well, I gotta go. See ya later."

"Knock 'em dead," said Mr. Critter without looking up from his paper.

"Why would you want LC to do that?" asked Little Sister. "I thought you said fighting was bad."

"It's just an expression," explained Mrs. Critter. "It doesn't have anything to do with fighting. It means to try really hard, to show everybody how good you are."

"That doesn't make any sense," said Little Sister, eating a big mouthful of her cereal. "Grown-up stuff never does."

LC walked down the driveway to his mailbox. Gabby wasn't there. LC looked over at Gabby's house just as she came running across her yard.

"Sorry I'm late," said Gabby. "I just finished the cover of my report. I drew a picture of Amelia Critterhart. You know, she disappeared trying to fly her plane around the world."

"Did she crash?" asked LC.

"I don't know," said Gabby. "It's one of the biggest mysteries of all time."

LC grinned. Gabby loved mysteries. That's why she started the Critter Kids Detective Club.

LC whistled as they walked down Green Frog Lane.

"Why are you in such a good mood?" asked Gabby.

"No reason," said LC. "I just wrote the best report ever."

"Who'd you do your report about?" Gabby asked.

"Cornelius Van der Critter," said LC. "He founded the town of Critterville."

"Is he related to mean old Miss Van der Critter?" asked Gabby.

"Yep," LC said as they walked along

Main Street. "She's his great-grand-daughter. Only he was really nice."

"That's hard to believe," said Gabby. "Miss Van der Critter is probably the meanest critter on the planet."

"I know," said LC. "But listen to all the nice stuff he did." LC opened his knapsack and pulled out his report. He flipped to the last page as he and Gabby walked by Shadow Close.

Just then a cloud covered the sun and it got dark outside. The wind began to blow. The trees bent back in the wind and leaves blew across their path.

"Hey, where'd all this wind come from?" Gabby asked as her hair blew into her eyes.

"Beats me," said LC. Then before he knew what had happened, his report was blown right out of his hands and down Shadow Close.

"Oh, no!" yelled LC. "My report! We've got to get it!"

LC and Gabby ran down the block as fast as they could go. But no matter how fast they ran, they couldn't catch LC's report. It kept blowing farther and farther away. They followed it to the end of Shadow Close, where the road came to a dead end.

"There it is!" yelled Gabby, pointing to some white papers stuck in the fence of the very last house on Shadow Close.

LC ran toward the fence. Just as he tried to grab the papers, another gust of wind came and blew them right up to the front door of the house.

"I have to get my report," said LC, "or I'm gonna be in big trouble."

"But you know what they say about this house," said Gabby. "It's haunted."

"I don't care," LC said. "I have to get that report." LC opened the gate. Suddenly the front door of the house swung open.

"Did you see that?" whispered Gabby, her eyes wide.

"Uh-huh," whispered LC.

They stood together staring at the house. Just then the wind picked up again and blew LC's report right into the haunted house. Before they could blink, the door mysteriously slammed shut.

"Aaahhhhhh!" LC and Gabby screamed.

"It's the ghost!" yelled Gabby.

LC and Gabby ran away from the house as fast as they could. They didn't stop running until they got to Critterville Elementary. Just then the late bell rang.

"Oh, no," said Gabby. "We're late."

"And I don't have my report," said LC. "I'm really in for it now."

LC and Gabby raced into their classroom. All the kids in their class were already there and Mr. Hogwash was standing by his desk. He was frowning.

"Ah, Mr. Critter, Miss Gump," began Mr. Hogwash. "How nice of you to join us. Your reports please."

Gabby opened her knapsack and pulled out her report. She handed it to Mr. Hogwash. "You can sit down now, Miss Gump," said Mr. Hogwash. "And your report, Mr. Critter," said Mr. Hogwash, turning to LC.

"Ummm . . . it . . . I mean . . . I . . ." stammered LC.

"You mean you don't have your report," said Mr. Hogwash.

"It blew away on my way to school," said LC.

"Next time you'll tell me your dog ate it," said Mr. Hogwash. "Anyway, there is no wind to speak of today."

"It's true, Mr. Hogwash," said Gabby. "Honest. We were walking together and LC's report suddenly blew into the haunted house on Shadow Close. The ghost got it."

"Come, come," said Mr. Hogwash. "There are no such things as ghosts. Listen

to me very carefully, Mr. Critter. It's Friday morning. I expect that report on my desk first thing Monday morning. Or else."

LC walked slowly to his seat. He was in big trouble now. He either had to go back to the haunted house and face the ghost or rewrite his entire report. He didn't know which was worse.

CHAPTER 3

THE GHOST STRIKES AGAIN

When school was over, LC walked slowly over to the lockers. The rest of the Critter Kids were already there, packing up their books. Tiger, LC's best friend, was twirling a basketball on the end of his finger.

"Dude," said Tiger. "Wanna shoot some hoops?"

"I can't," said LC.

"He has to rewrite his report," said Gabby from her locker, which was right next to LC's. "And I bet it takes all weekend to do it."

"But I don't think I can rewrite it," said LC. "It'll never be as good as the first one."

"Forget redoing it," said Tiger. "We'll go get it right now."

"I don't think that's such a good idea," said Gabby. "That report was sucked right through the front door of the haunted house. It was definitely the ghost."

"I bet it was just the wind," said Henrietta, dribbling the ball away from Tiger. Henrietta was a great b-ball player. She was queen of the slam dunk.

"No, it wasn't," said Gabby. "I was there. I saw it with my very own eyes."

"There are no such things as ghosts," said Su Su. "Everybody knows that."

"Yeah, dude," said Tiger. "We'll go get your report right now."

"Don't worry," said Gator, LC's other best friend.

"Wait till we get there," said Gabby. "You'll see."

"Come on, guys," said Henrietta. "Let's do the Critter Kid Shake for good luck."

They all did the Critter Kid Shake. LC followed his friends down the front steps of the school. He hoped they were right and there was no ghost. But he couldn't help remembering the way that door had opened and closed all by itself. LC had never seen the wind do anything like that before. It was really spooky.

The Critter Kids walked down Main Street toward Shadow Close.

"We're almost there," said Gabby.

"Cool," said Tiger.

"There it is," said LC, pointing to the house at the end of the street.

"No problem," said Tiger, bouncing his basketball along as he walked. "It looks like an ordinary house to me."

LC had to admit the house didn't look very haunted in the bright sunlight. Maybe he and Gabby had been imagining things.

They stopped in front of the house. Suddenly the gate banged open in the wind, just as the sun slipped behind the clouds, leaving the house in shadow.

"This house gives me the creeps," said Su Su, shivering.

"See what I mean," said Gabby.

"Yeah," said Velvet, her eyes wide.

"Come on," said Tiger. "There are no such things as ghosts, remember?"

"Well, actually, parapsychologists have discovered that apparitions, or poltergeists—what we call ghosts—may in fact exist," said Timothy.

"Let's go ring the doorbell," said Tiger.

Nobody said anything as they followed Tiger into the yard of the haunted house.

"Are you sure we should do this?" whispered Velvet.

The Critter Kids walked slowly up the front steps of the house. Suddenly the front door swung open.

"Who opened the door?" asked Tiger.

"I thought you did," said LC.

"If LC didn't open the door and you didn't open the door, then who did?" Gabby asked Tiger.

"I guess it opened by itself," said Tiger.

"It's probably just one of those electronic doors, like in the supermarket."

"In an old house?" said Su Su. "I don't think so."

"Don't worry," said Tiger, walking into the house. The Critter Kids followed him into the front hall.

"Gross!" said Su Su. "Look at all those cobwebs!"

"I think we should get out of here," said Gabby.

"Me too," said Velvet. "It's really creepy in here."

LC gulped and looked around him. The furniture was covered with white sheets and there was dust everywhere. "I don't know about this, Tiger," he said.

"It's cool," said Tiger. He took another step into the room. Just then a chandelier crashed to the floor right in front of them!

"Aaaahhhh!!!!" everybody screamed.

They turned and ran out of the house as

fast as they could. When they got to the clubhouse, they all plopped down on chairs to catch their breath.

"We told you it was a ghost," said Gabby.

"You were right," said Gator.

"Totally," agreed Tiger.

LC sighed. "Now I'm never gonna get my report," he said.

Nobody said anything for a minute.

"That's not true," said Timothy suddenly. He stood up and walked over to the chalkboard in the back of the room. "Not true at all."

Everyone stared at him.

"All we need to do is find the exact location of the ghost," Timothy said.

"How do we do that?" asked Velvet.

"Simply by measuring the levels of electromagnetic force," explained Timothy. "Ghosts generate huge amounts of the stuff."

"Huh?" said Henrietta, stuffing three

chocolate peanut butter cookies into her mouth.

The Kids looked at each other. No one knew what Timothy was talking about.

"Once we locate the area inside the house where there is a high level of electromagnetic force," Timothy said, "that is, where the ghost is, then . . ." He paused and looked around the table.

"Then what?" asked Gabby.

"Then we can trap the ghost," said Timothy.

"With what?" asked LC.

"With ghost-fighting equipment," Timothy said. "That's what."

"How are we gonna get ghost-fighting equipment?" asked Gator. "I bet it's really expensive."

"Yeah," agreed Henrietta, her mouth full of chocolate and peanut butter.

"Don't worry," said Timothy. "We can make our own ghost-fighting equipment. I'll write up a list of what we need."

"This is great!" said Gabby. "We'll be the ghost-fighters of Critterville!"

CHAPTER 4

TO CATCH A GHOST

The next morning was Saturday. Instead of watching his favorite cartoon, "X-Critter," LC got right to work. He pulled his first piece of ghost-fighting equipment out of the hall closet. Just then someone rang the doorbell three times in a row.

"Come in, Tiger," called LC. LC knew it was Tiger. He always rang the bell three times fast.

"Dude," said Tiger, "sure hope your mom says we can have that, 'cuz my mom said no way."

"No problem," said LC. "My dad just bought this. It'll be perfect. It even has a headlight. Grab the other end."

Tiger and LC dragged the vacuum cleaner out to the Critters' front yard. Mr. Critter and Little Sister were kneeling in the grass, weeding his dad's prize pumpkin patch.

"Hey, Dad," said LC. "Can I borrow the vacuum cleaner?"

"Don't give it to him, Dad," said Little Sister. "He's up to something."

"We need it for a school project, Mr. Critter," said Tiger with his best smile.

"Well, if it's for a school project then I guess so," said Mr. Critter. "Just don't forget to change the bag."

"Thanks, Dad," said LC.

LC and Tiger dragged the vacuum cleaner around the house to the backyard. Little Sister was right behind them. Mrs. Critter was sitting on the Critters' tractor mower. She had just finished mowing.

"Cool mower, Mrs. Critter," said Tiger.

"Hey, Mom, can we borrow the battery from the mower?" asked LC.

"Yeah," said Tiger. "We need it for a science project."

"Okay," said Mrs. Critter, hopping off the mower and pulling out the battery. "But be careful with it."

"Thanks, Mom," said LC, taking the battery. He and Tiger dragged the battery and the vacuum cleaner away.

"You can kiss that battery good-bye," said Little Sister to Mrs. Critter.

While everyone collected ghost-fighting materials, Timothy was busy creating the "Ultimate Electromagnetic Poltergeist Detection and Removal System." He was in his bedroom making complicated calculations on his computer when LC and Tiger got there.

"Ah, a fine specimen," said Timothy as he

examined the vacuum cleaner.

Just then someone knocked on the door. It was Su Su. She dumped a bunch of blow-dryers on Timothy's bed.

"What are you doing with that vacuum cleaner?" she asked.

"Once we locate the electromagnetic disturbance, we'll be able to suck it in and trap it inside this electronic refuse container," said Timothy.

"Well, just be careful with my blow-dryers," said Su Su. "I've got to go meet Gator and Velvet."

"What are the dryers for?" asked Tiger.

"We're going to attach them to the battery packs," said Timothy. "I'll reverse the electrons, causing them to give off a powerful electric pulse which will help direct the poltergeist right into the trap."

Su Su met Gator and Velvet at the Critterville Five and Ten. Velvet was pushing a cart filled with boxes of tinfoil and plastic goggles.

"What's all that stuff for?" asked Su Su.

"The goggles are to protect our eyes in case the ghost shoots any ectoplasm at us," said Velvet.

"Hey, here are the oven mitts," said Gator, throwing a few pairs into the cart.

"Better get a few more," added Velvet, tossing some extra pairs into the cart.

"What for?" asked Su Su.

"To protect our hands," said Gator. "Ectoplasm is kind of sticky."

"Gross," said Su Su, picking up a lipstick and putting some on her lips. "How does this color look on me?" she asked.

"Fine, I guess," said Velvet. "But I don't think ghosts care boo about lipstick."

Gator laughed as they pushed the cart over to the checkout counter.

"Well, I do," said Su Su. "And by the way, I wouldn't be caught dead in those oven mitts and goggles."

After they paid for all the stuff, Gator, Velvet, and Su Su went to Timothy's house. Everyone was there except for Gabby and Henrietta.

"I wonder what's taking them so long at the town hall," said LC.

Just then Gabby and Henrietta ran into the room. "Listen to this," said Gabby. "We looked up who lived in the haunted house."

"You'll never believe who it belonged to," added Henrietta, taking a big bite out of her pastrami club sandwich.

"Who?" asked LC.

"Cornelius Van der Critter," said Gabby. "That's who."

"The same Cornelius Van der Critter I did my report about?" asked LC, his eyes wide.

"Yep," said Gabby. "The exact same one."

CHAPTER 5

GHOST FIGHTERS

After dinner the Critter Kids met at the clubhouse. Ghost-fighting equipment was piled up everywhere.

"Okay, Gabby and Tiger, you suit up first," said Timothy.

"Goggles, gloves, helmets," Velvet read aloud from the list Timothy had made.

"Check," said Tiger and Gabby as they put bicycle helmets on their heads, oven

mitts on their hands, and plastic goggles over their eyes.

"Battery packs," said Velvet.

"Check," said Tiger and Gabby as they each took a knapsack with a battery inside and put it on their backs.

"Blow-dryers," said Velvet.

"Check," said Tiger and Gabby as they each grabbed a blow-dryer from the table.

"Okay, you two are ready to go," said Timothy. "Everyone else get dressed—except you, LC."

"Don't I get to wear any of that stuff?" asked LC.

"Yes," said Timothy. "But first you have to put on the proton-proof silver suit."

"Why?" asked LC as Timothy began to wrap tinfoil around him.

"Because you're the focus critter," said Timothy. "It's highly probable the ghost will focus all its energies on you. And this suit is the only thing that will protect you."

"Nice outfit," said Henrietta, grinning.

When the Critter Kids were all set, they marched down Green Frog Lane and headed for Shadow Close. Gabby and Henrietta led the way with flashlights. Tiger and Gator pulled Mr. Critter's vacuum cleaner while Timothy wheeled his computer equipment along in a wagon.

They had to go slowly because if LC walked too fast, his proton-proof suit started to fall off.

"I bet that ghost takes one look at us and gets so scared he runs away," said Tiger.

"Yeah," said LC as they finally turned down Shadow Close.

Suddenly a flash of lightning lit up the sky right behind the haunted house.

"Maybe this isn't such a good idea after all," said Gabby.

"Yeah, maybe we should come back some other time," said Henrietta.

"No," said Timothy, punching some keys on his computer. "This is perfect. There's a high level of electromagnetic force concentrated inside the house. The ghost is there. And we're gonna get it!"

Timothy led everyone around to the back of the house. "All right," he said. "We're going in through the basement."

"Why?" asked LC.

"Because it's the best way to flush out the ghost," said Timothy. "We'll drive him from the bottom of the house to the top. Then we'll trap him upstairs in the attic."

"What about the door?" asked Tiger. "It's locked."

Without a word, Timothy ran over to the door, jumped in the air, and kicked it wide open. "Ghost-fighters, let's do it!" he said.

CHAPTER 6

GHOST ENCOUNTERS

"We better split up," said Timothy as soon as they got inside. "LC and Gabby, you take the stairs. Everyone else, spread out."

LC and Gabby began walking up the stairs. Suddenly there was a loud humming sound coming from the back of the basement. LC and Gabby turned around.

"We've got it covered," said Timothy. "You guys keep going. Okay, everybody, let's go get it."

Timothy and Tiger led the way through the basement. The humming sound grew louder and louder.

"On the count of three, we shoot," said Timothy. "One . . . two . . . three . . ."

The whole room lit up as everyone aimed and fired.

"Hold your fire!" Tiger yelled. "It's just the furnace."

"Okay, ghost-fighters," said Timothy. "Let's move out."

Meanwhile LC and Gabby were inching their way along the upstairs hallway.

"I wonder if they got the ghost," said Gabby, turning her head to look back at the stairs.

"I don't know," said LC. He turned the handle on the door next to him. It opened, so he stepped inside. *Whoosh!* The door suddenly shut behind him.

"Maybe we should go back," said Gabby. "I think we better find out what's going on down there, don't you, LC?"

There was no answer. Gabby spun around. LC was nowhere in sight.

"Aaahhh!" screamed Gabby. "The ghost got LC!" She turned on her ghost-fighting gear and fired into the darkness.

At the same time LC tried to open the door to get back to the hallway, but it was stuck. There was no way out. LC shined his flashlight around. He spotted a stairway in the corner.

Slowly, LC made his way toward it. He saw light coming from underneath the door at the top of the stairs. He turned on his ghost-fighting equipment and inched his way up to the door.

Suddenly the door swung open.

LC could feel his heart pounding as he walked into a small room. There, floating above a big wooden desk, was something that made his heart beat even faster—it was the ghost.

"Good evening, Mr. Critter," said the ghost as he sank down into a chair. "I've been expecting you. Have a seat and please turn off that contraption. It's giving me a headache."

LC sat down and turned off his gear.

"First of all, there are many spelling mistakes in your report," said the ghost. "Other than that, I think it's pretty good. I'm glad to hear that the folks in Critterville think so highly of me."

"You mean *you're* Cornelius Van der Critter?" said LC, staring at the ghost.

"Why, of course," said the ghost. "Who else would I be? Anyway, I'm glad you're finally here because there's something very important I need you to do for me."

"There is?" asked LC.

The ghost pulled a yellowed piece of parchment paper from the top drawer of his desk. He handed it to LC. "This is my will," said the ghost. "I died before I could give it to my lawyer. I need you to take it to my law firm immediately. They'll know what to do with it. My great-grand-daughter Petunia Van der Critter is in for a big surprise."

"You mean Miss Van der Critter's name is Petunia?!" exclaimed LC.

Just then the Critter Kids burst into the room.

"Who in the world were you talking to?" asked Gabby.

"Cornelius Van der Critter," said LC.

"But there's nobody here," said Tiger.

"Are you trying to tell me you were having a conversation with a ghost?" asked Gabby.

"Yes," said LC. "He gave me back my

report and then he gave me this will. He wants me to get it to a lawyer right away."

The Critter Kids all looked at the piece of paper in LC's hand. It said: "Last Will and Testament of Cornelius Van der Critter."

"Hey, what's all that stuff?" asked Gator, pointing to some green slime that was stuck to the empty chair and desk.

"I believe that's ectoplasm," said Timothy, collecting some in a jar.

"I told you the ghost was here," said LC. "I told you."

CHAPTER 7

WHERE THERE'S A WILL, THERE'S A WAY

The next morning LC and the Critter Kids took Cornelius Van der Critter's will down to the Main Street offices of Skunk and Weasel, Attorneys at Law. LC knocked on the door. There was no answer.

"I told you they weren't going to be open," said Gabby. "It's Sunday."

"I know, but Mr. Van der Critter told me to take care of it right away," said LC. He knocked again.

Just then someone came to the window.

"Go away! We're closed!" called a grumpy voice.

"We need a lawyer," shouted LC.

"What do you kids need a lawyer for?" asked the grumpy voice.

"We have something from Mr. Cornelius Van der Critter," shouted Gabby.

Suddenly the door opened.

"I'm a lawyer. Smelly's the name," said a chubby critter with a pair of glasses on his nose. He stared at the Critter Kids. "And that's impossible. Cornelius Van der Critter died over a hundred years ago."

LC didn't say anything. He just handed the will to Mr. Smelly. Mr. Smelly stared at the will. Then he frowned at the Kids. Then he stared at the will again.

"Come with me," he said as he led the way into his office. He went to his desk and opened the top drawer. He pulled out a large magnifying glass and peered at the signature at the bottom of the will.

"Hmmmmm," said Mr. Smelly. "Now, how exactly did you kids come by this will?" he finally asked, staring at the Critter Kids over the top of his glasses.

"The ghost gave it to me, sir," said LC.

"Ghost?!" said Mr. Smelly.

"Yeah, Mr. Van der Critter's ghost," said LC. "He lives in the haunted house at the end of Shadow Close." LC told Mr. Smelly all about his history report and how he and the Critter Kids had gone into the house to get it back.

"Hmmmm," murmured Mr. Smelly again as he stared at the will.

"I told you it was a fake," said Su Su.

"Not at all," said Mr. Smelly. "Ghost or no ghost, this is indeed the missing last will and testament of Cornelius Van der Critter. Some critters, who shall remain unnamed for the present time, are in for quite a shock!"

"What do you mean?" asked Gabby.

"You kids wait here," said Mr. Smelly. "I have to make some phone calls."

A few hours later Miss Petunia Van der Critter came charging into Mr. Smelly's office.

"How dare you interrupt me at my

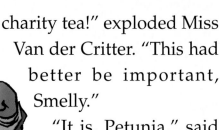

charity tea!" exploded Miss Van der Critter. "This had better be important, Smelly."

"It is, Petunia," said Mr. Smelly. "Have a seat."

"Well, let's get on with it," said Miss Van der Critter. "They're waiting for me at the club."

Miss Van der Critter looked at the Critter Kids. "What are *they* doing here?" she barked.

The Critter Kids didn't say anything.

"Just sit down, Petunia," said Mr. Smelly.

At that moment the door opened again. Rocky and his mom walked in.

"Excuse me," said Rocky. "Is this Mr. Smelly's office?"

"Yes, Rocky," said Mr. Smelly. "Why don't you and your mother have a seat."

"Harrumph," sputtered Miss Van der

Critter. "That's the boy I had fired from the market. What in the world is *he* doing here? I simply won't have this!"

"Now that we're all here," Mr. Smelly said, "it's time to begin."

"This better be good," said Miss Van der Critter.

"Oh, it is, Petunia," said Mr. Smelly with a smile. "It seems that a long time ago your great-grandfather, Cornelius Van der Critter, had a son. This son grew up and had a son.

And then this son, your father, had a son and a daughter."

"Get to the point!" shouted Miss Van der Critter. "I know my family history."

"You, Petunia, are, of course, the daughter," said Mr. Smelly. "But if you remember, you also had a brother."

Miss Van der Critter sank back in her seat. "Oh, yes, that's true," she said with a sigh. "My long-lost brother, Rockwell, who ran away from home and was never heard

from again. I miss him so."

"Well, meet your brother's son—Rockwell the second," said Mr. Smelly, pointing to Rocky. "Your nephew is entitled to exactly one half of your fortune according to your great-grandfather's will, which has just now been found."

Petunia Van der Critter didn't say a word. She hit the floor with a thud.

"She's out cold," said LC.

"Serves her right," said Gabby.

"Wow! Rocky! Now you can go to college," said LC.

"Do you think I can get my job back at Mr. Muncher's?" asked Rocky.

"Not only that," said Mr. Smelly. "You can buy that market if you want to."

"Yay!" shouted all the Critter Kids.

"I'll call the newspaper," said Mr. Smelly. "This will be big news all over Critterville."

The next morning LC left early for school. He was so early he decided to stop by Muncher's Market for a muffin.

When he got there, he saw Mr. Hogwash.

"Hi, Mr. Hogwash," said LC. "Here's my report."

"Thank you, Mr. Critter," said Mr.

Hogwash. "But I've already read it."

He handed LC his newspaper. On the front page, next to a picture of Cornelius Van der Critter, was LC's report.

LC couldn't believe it!

"Good work, Mr. Critter," said Mr. Hogwash.

"A fine job," said a voice from behind LC.

"Thanks to you, I have been reunited with my family."

LC turned around. It was Miss Van der Critter.

"Aunt Petunia," said Rocky, "here's your chocolate chip muffin. It's the last one!"

"Rockwell, dear, I've changed my mind," said Miss Van der Critter. "This muffin is for LC. Charge it to my account."

LC smiled as he took a big bite of the chocolate chip muffin. He had a feeling that the ghost of Shadow Close was just as happy as he was.